Meet the Kreeps

Kicking and Screaming

Meet the Kreeps

Meet the Kreeps

Kicking and Screaming

by Kiki Thorpe

Scholastic Inc.

New York • Toronto • London • Auckland
Sydney • Mexico City • New Delhi • Hong Kong

No part of this publication may be reproduced, stored in
a retrieval system, or transmitted in any form or by any
means, electronic, mechanical, photocopying, recording,
or otherwise, without written permission of the publisher.
For information regarding permission, write to
Scholastic, Inc., Attention: Permissions Department,
557 Broadway, New York, NY 10012.

ISBN-13: 978-0-545-13171-1
ISBN-10: 0-545-13171-5

12 11 10 9 8 7 6 5 4 3 2 1   9 10 11 12 13 14/0

Printed in the U.S.A.
First printing, November 2009

For Axel and Udo

❧ Chapter 1 ❧

Polly Winkler pushed open the rusty gate of the dark old mansion. She darted past the Venus flytraps and poison toadstools in the front yard and dashed up the splintery front steps. Tugging open the heavy front door, Polly slipped into the tomb-like darkness of the house, calling out, "Dad! I'm home!"

"In the kitchen, kiddo!" Dr. Winkler hollered back.

Polly hurried to the kitchen. Her dad was sitting at the table, reading a newspaper. Polly's five-year-old stepsister, Esme, was sitting next to him, drawing, and Polly's stepmother, Veronica, was stirring something in a cauldron on the stove.

Polly stood up very straight and asked them, "Do you notice anything different about me?"

"Well, let's see," said her dad, putting down his paper. "Did you change your hair?"

Polly smiled. "Nope."

Veronica tapped her long red fingernails against the stove thoughtfully. "I know. You changed your nose!"

Polly giggled. "No. They measured us in health class today and —"

"Dad!" Polly's older sister, Joy, suddenly burst into the room. "You'll never guess what happened today!" she screeched.

Dr. Winkler stroked his mustache. "Well, let's see —"

"I made captain of the cheerleading team! Yay!" Joy kicked her leg in the air.

"That's terrific, honey," Dr. Winkler said.

"Cool!" Polly exclaimed.

"Wonderful, darling," Veronica added. "What exactly does a cheerleading captain do?"

"It's a really big deal," Joy told her. "I get to start off all the cheers. And I'm always at the top of the human pyramid. But it's not all fun stuff like that. It's also a big responsibility. I have to make up cheers, too. I've been working on one today. . . . Listen to this."

Joy got into position and began. *"Go, go, Mad Dogs . . . !"*

Polly waited for her to go on. But Joy just dropped her arms and smiled. "What do you think?"

"It's good," said Dr. Winkler. "Though maybe a little short."

"Oh, there's more to it than that," Joy said. "I just haven't come up with it yet. I've been working on it all afternoon." Her big blue eyes widened. "What if I can't think of the rest of the words? I'd be letting the whole team down!"

"Did someone say 'words'?" asked Polly's younger brother, Petey, walking in at that moment.

"Oh, Petey!" Joy grabbed his arm. "Thank goodness! You can help me. You know lots of words!"

"That's true. I *am* the Endsville Elementary spelling bee champion," Petey said proudly, polishing his glasses on his shirt.

Polly rolled her eyes. Petey never missed a chance to remind people that he'd won the school spelling bee.

Just then, the doorbell rang. Polly's dad went to answer it. A second later, he called, "Veronica, dear? You'd better come here!"

Veronica went to the door with Polly, Joy, and Esme following curiously. There on the doorstep stood Veronica's oldest son, Vincent. Standing on either side of him were two police officers.

"Is this the Kreep-Winkler household?" one of the policemen asked.

"Yes, I'm Wally Winkler," said Polly's dad. "And this is my wife, Veronica Kreep. What's going on?"

"Earlier this afternoon, your son was skating in the Endsville cemetery," the policeman said.

"Oh, Vincent." Veronica sighed. "I've told you over and over — graveyards aren't safe during the daytime!"

The officer held up a hand. "Let me

finish, ma'am. While he was in a remote part of the grounds, your son came across a mugger bothering an old woman who was visiting her husband's grave."

"Vincent skated right into the attacker and knocked him down," the other officer said. "Your son is a hero."

"A hero?" said Polly's dad. "Well, I'll be. That's amazing news!"

"Certainly unexpected," Veronica agreed happily.

"We just wanted to thank you personally for raising such a fine boy," the first officer said. "Now, we'd better be going. Some joker has been setting off missiles in the neighborhood. You haven't seen anything suspicious, have you?"

"I don't think so. Did you say *missiles*?" asked Polly's dad.

The officer nodded. "So far, they're harmless, but people are getting upset. We're on the case." The policemen tipped their caps and left.

Dr. Winkler shut the door behind them. Everyone crowded around Vincent, congratulating him. "Way to go!" "Nicely done, son." "A hero. Cool!"

The telephone rang, interrupting them. Joy went to answer it. "Just a minute," she said, her eyes widening again.

"Who is it?" asked Dr. Winkler.

Joy looked a little stunned. "It's NASA!"

"NASA? What could they want?" Dr. Winkler reached for the phone, but Joy shook her head.

"It's not for you. It's for Damon!" she said.

Suddenly, the door to the basement burst open, and Polly's other stepbrother, Damon, appeared in a cloud of smoke. He was wearing goggles and a chemical-stained lab coat.

"I'll take that!" Damon yanked the cord-less phone from Joy's grip. A second later, he had disappeared back into his basement laboratory.

"Imagine that," Polly's dad said, scratching his head. "NASA calling for Damon."

"I always said he was a genius," Veronica replied.

"Mummy," said a small voice. Esme was tugging at Veronica's skirt. She held up a piece of paper. "Look at the picture I made."

Veronica took the drawing. "Darling! How gorgeous!" she exclaimed.

Polly peered over her shoulder. The picture wasn't just gorgeous — it was amazing! Esme had drawn the Kreeps' mansion using nothing but teeny-tiny black dots. Every detail was perfect, right down to the bats hanging from the eaves.

"Esme, did you do this all by yourself?" Polly's dad asked in astonishment.

"Bubbles helped," said Esme, holding up her pet tarantula. The spider's feet were covered in ink. "She did all the dots. But I told her where to go."

Veronica scooped Esme up and planted a kiss on her cheek. "My brilliant little girl! You're good at art *and* spiders."

Polly's dad beamed and put his arm around Veronica. "What a bunch of talented kids!"

Just then, his eyes fell on Polly. "I'm sorry, honey. There was something you wanted to tell me before. What was it?" he asked.

Polly ducked her head. Suddenly, her news — that she'd grown one whole inch — didn't seem so important. "Never mind," she told her dad.

Polly looked around at her brothers and sisters. They were all so talented and amazing and heroic. Not like Polly.

I'm just plain old Polly, she thought. *One inch taller, and not very special at all.*

⊁ Chapter 2 ⊀

"M ike, do you think I'm good at anything?" Polly asked her best friend
the next afternoon.

The two friends were kicking a soccer
ball back and forth in Mike's backyard.
"Sure," said Mike, receiving Polly's pass.
"You're good at lots of things."

"Like what?" Polly asked.

Mike juggled the ball with his feet, thinking. "Well, you're fun to hang out with. And
you have lots of funny ideas."

"But is there something I'm *really* good
at?" Polly wondered. "So if someone asked
about me, you would say, 'Polly Winkler is

11

the best artist I know.' Or, 'Polly Winkler is so smart she ought to work for NASA'?"

Mike stopped the ball under one foot and squinted at Polly. "What are you talking about?"

Polly sighed. "I'm talking about my brothers and sisters. They all have talents that make them special. But I'm not good at anything."

"Sure you are," said Mike, kicking the ball back to her.

"Name one thing."

"I don't know." Mike shrugged. "You're just good at being Polly!"

"Hmph," said Polly. That wasn't the answer she was looking for.

Suddenly, Polly felt angry. *Why should Joy and Petey and Vincent and Damon and even little Esme get to be so special?* she thought. *Why should they get all the attention?*

12

"It's not fair!" Polly grumbled, and drawing back her foot, she booted the ball as hard as she could.

The ball sailed up and over Mike's fence, into the neighbor's yard. Mike gave a long whistle. "Wow!" he said. "That was some kick!"

"It was pretty good, wasn't it?" Polly said, surprised. She'd never kicked the ball that far before.

"You should think about joining a soccer team," Mike said. "The community center is starting a free team for boys and girls. I'm going to sign up. You could, too!"

Polly frowned. "I don't know, Mike. I've never played soccer anywhere but in your yard."

"That doesn't matter. It's just for fun," Mike told her.

Polly looked over the fence, to where

the ball had gone. "You really think I'd be good?"

"With a kick like that? You're a natural!" said Mike.

Polly thought about that. Maybe Mike was on to something. Maybe she did have a talent after all. A hidden talent for soccer!

"Okay," she told Mike. "Count me in!"

"Cool," Mike said, slapping her a high five. "You won't be sorry. We're going to have a blast!"

Later that night, Polly's family sat around the table under the spider-shaped chandelier in the dining room. As Polly's dad carved a roasted chicken, Veronica passed around bowls of strange, slippery green vegetables. As usual, there was a lot of noise and chatter and things knocked over as the food was handed around.

Polly cleared her throat. "I have an announcement," she told her family.

But no one seemed to hear. "Veronica, dear, are you *sure* the butcher said this was chicken?" Dr. Winkler asked, studying the meat he was cutting.

"Why do you ask?" Veronica wondered.

"It's just that it seems to have *four* drum-sticks rather than two," said Polly's dad.

"Oh, I always buy chicken that way," Veronica replied. "The more legs, the better! Wouldn't you agree?"

"I like legs," Joy agreed cheerily.

"Personally, I prefer the neck," said Vincent.

Polly sighed and tried again, louder. "I *said* I have an announcement."

Her dad finally looked up from the chicken. "What announcement?" he asked.

Polly sat up importantly in her seat. "I've decided to start a new activity."

"That's great, honey!" her dad replied enthusiastically. "I've always said, a person without a hobby is like a ham loaf without pineapple. So, what will it be? If you ever want advice on stamp collecting, you know who to come to," he added with a wink.

"*Dad*," said Joy, rolling her eyes. "Stamp collecting is for nerds. What Polly wants is a *fun* hobby — like cheerleading!"

"Cheerleading?" Vincent scoffed. "That's about as fun as a trip to the dentist. Sorry, Wally," he added with a glance at Dr. Winkler, who *was* a dentist.

Vincent turned to Polly. "You should take up skateboarding. It's the greatest sport known to humankind. Or *in*humankind," he added.

"Or science!" Damon chimed in, waving a half-chewed drumstick. "You can be the subject of my next experiment. Make scientific history! Now *that's* what I call thrilling!"

Suddenly, the whole family was talking over one another, suggesting different hobbies for Polly.

"What about sword swallowing?"

"Crossword puzzles are fun!"

"Try taxidermy!"

"Have you considered levitation?"

"Wait, wait!" Polly held up her hands. "I already *have* a hobby. What I'm trying to tell you is, I joined a soccer team!"

"Soccer, you say?" asked her dad.

"Soccer. S-o-c-c-e-r," Petey declared. "'A game played on a field between two teams who score by kicking a ball.'"

"Thank you, Petey," Dr. Winkler said

with a little smile. "I *know* what soccer is. I just didn't know that Polly was interested in it."

"Mike told me about a free team starting at the community center. I signed up for it today."

Polly had expected congratulations or at least some sort of encouragement. But her family had all gone back to eating. They didn't seem very interested in soccer.

"I think it sounds nice," piped up a small voice from near Polly's elbow.

Polly looked over and saw Esme smiling up at her. *At least* someone *appreciates me*, she thought.

"Soccer is the game where they use a head for the ball. And the losers get sacrificed, right?" asked Esme.

"No, Esme," Damon replied. "You're

thinking of *pitz*, the game of the ancient Mayans."

"Oh, yeah. *Pitz*." Esme frowned. "That's too bad. I always wanted to see a real human sacrifice."

"Not until you're older, dear," Veronica said.

Polly looked around the table. Wasn't anyone in this crazy family interested in her hobby?

"What's the name of your team, Polly?" asked Veronica as she began to clear away the empty plates.

"The Dust Devils," Polly replied. "But just the Devils, for short."

"That's a lovely name!" Veronica stacked the plates on top of each other and started to head toward the kitchen. "I think that calls for some dessert! Who's ready for a piece of poisonberry pie?"

"I am!" "Me!" "Make mine with ice cream!" came the chorus of voices around the table. And just like that, everyone had forgotten about Polly and soccer.

It doesn't matter, Polly told herself. *Just wait until I start playing. Then they'll all see what a star I can be!*

✤ Chapter 3 ✤

The next week, on a sunny afternoon, Polly, Mike, and a group of other kids met in the big field behind the Endsville Community Center.

"Welcome to the first practice of the Dust Devils," boomed a stout woman holding a clipboard. "I'm Coach Kleet."

The coach wore a yellow sun visor, a whistle around her neck, and a wide, warm smile. Polly liked her right away.

"I have just a few things to cover," the coach told the team. "And then we can start playing!"

A boy with straw-colored hair raised his hand. "My name's Lukas," he said. "If you're going to assign positions now, I want to be center striker. I always play center striker."

"Everyone will get to try different positions before we decide," the coach replied. "But Lukas brings up a good question. Who here has played team soccer before?"

A dozen hands shot into the air. Polly looked around. She was the only one who hadn't raised her hand.

The coach squinted down at her. "Never played before?"

Polly blushed. "No, ma'am."

"Call me Coach," said the coach. "And don't worry. You'll be playing like a pro in no time."

Mike nudged Polly. "See?" he whispered. "What did I tell you?"

For the next few minutes, the coach took

attendance. Then she told everyone to line up for a dribbling drill.

As Polly got into line, Lukas cut in front of her. "Beginners go to the back of the line," he sneered.

"I'm not a beginner," Polly said, lifting her chin. "I know how to play."

"Oh, yeah? Only a newbie would wear *basketball* shoes on a *soccer* field," Lukas said, pointing at Polly's feet.

Polly looked down at her beat-up sneakers. They were the ones she wore every day. Looking around, she realized that all the other kids had on soccer cleats. Polly felt embarrassed. She'd already goofed, and practice hadn't even started yet!

"Last year, my team took second place in the league," Lukas said, putting his face right up close to Polly's. "This year, I want to win. And no beginner is going to mess it up for me."

"You don't have to worry about Polly," Mike said, jumping to her defense. "She's really good. You should have seen her boot the ball over the fence in my backyard."

"This isn't your backyard," Lukas shot back. "This is *real* soccer." With that, he took off dribbling the ball.

"Don't worry about him," Mike told Polly. "He thinks he's some kind of hotshot."

"Maybe he is," Polly said. She watched Lukas deftly weave the ball between a row of orange cones. "He looks pretty good to me. You can't blame him for wanting to win."

Mike shrugged. "Winning isn't everything."

When it was Polly's turn, she tried to dribble through the cones the way she'd seen Lukas do. But it wasn't easy. She couldn't make the ball go exactly where she wanted. It didn't help that Lukas was watching.

"You're supposed to dribble between the cones, not *through* them," he sneered when Polly knocked one over.

Polly tried to ignore him. But after that, things seemed to go even worse. Polly ran the wrong way in a passing drill. She tripped over the ball in a sprinting exercise. She slipped in a scrimmage and hit her elbow so hard it brought tears to her eyes.

"Maybe I made a mistake," Polly said as she and Mike walked home after practice. She rubbed her sore elbow. "Maybe soccer isn't the right hobby for me."

"Don't worry, you'll get the hang of it," Mike reassured her. "You just need the right shoes and stuff. Besides," he added, "you can't quit before we have a game. The games are the best part! When you're playing a game, everything just clicks. And when you score a goal, it's the greatest feeling in the world."

Polly tried to see herself scoring a goal. She imagined her family standing on the sidelines cheering her on. *That* would *be really cool,* she thought.

"I guess you're right, Mike," she said. "I can't quit yet."

"Just wait till we play our first game," Mike said. "You'll see. It's going to be great."

"I had my first soccer practice today," Polly announced at dinner that night.

"How did it go?" asked her dad as he chased a slippery piece of squid around his plate with a pair of chopsticks. Tonight the family was eating one of Veronica's secret recipes. She called it "Squid Surprise."

"Um, pretty good," Polly fibbed. "But I'm going to need to get some stuff — cleats and some shin guards and a pair of soccer shorts. Oh, and I need to bring twenty dollars to the next practice for my jersey."

Her dad choked on a piece of squid. Veronica had to whack him on the back. "Twenty dollars for a jersey?" he said, his eyes watering. "I thought this was supposed to be a *free* soccer team."

"Speaking of uniforms," Joy said to their father, "I need some money for new pompoms. My old ones have lost all their floof."

Damon cleared his throat. "While we're on the subject of money, now might be a good time to mention that I've had a high-powered radar antenna installed on the roof. You'll be getting a bill in the mail."

Dr. Winkler looked around at his children and stepchildren. "Do I look like a bank?" he asked.

Polly scowled at Joy and Damon. This time, she wasn't going to let them steal all

27

the attention. "Please?" she pleaded with her father. "It's really important. I can't play soccer without a uniform."

"And I can't cheer without floof!" said Joy.

Dr. Winkler gave a tired sigh. "Of course you can get a uniform, Polly. And you can get new pom-poms, Joy." He turned to Damon. "We'll discuss the antenna later."

"Thanks, Dad." Polly leaned back in her chair, relieved. "I need that stuff soon. The first game is a week from Saturday."

"A week from Saturday?" Dr. Winkler frowned. "Oh, no. That's the day of the Dismal Valley Dentist Conference. I'm giving an important talk. It's called 'Fillings Can Be Fun!'"

"But you have to come!" Polly exclaimed. "It's the first game of the season. All the other parents will be there."

"I wish I could. But I've got to fill a lot of cavities to keep up with you kids and your hobbies," he joked. "I'm sorry, Polly," he added when she didn't smile. "I promise I'll come to the next game."

"You know, I could come to your game, Polly," Veronica spoke up. "I promised I'd help at the Endsville Blood Drive that day. But I might be able to slip out early."

"That's okay, Veronica," said Polly with a heavy sigh. She couldn't believe that her dad wouldn't make it to her game. How could he be proud of her if he wouldn't even be there?

"Ahhh!" Petey suddenly screamed from down the table. Black ink dripped down his face. "My dinner just squirted me!"

"Oh, good!" Veronica clasped her hands together happily. "You found the Squid Surprise!"

As everyone's attention turned to Petey, Polly tried to swallow around the lump in her throat.

"It doesn't matter," she whispered to herself. Right then, Polly decided she would play better than ever. She would be the best soccer player that Endsville had ever seen. Then everyone would be sorry that they'd missed her game.

❈ Chapter 4 ❈

G ather up, Devils!" Coach Kleet hollered.

Polly kicked the ball into the net one last time, then jogged over to the coach. It was Saturday morning, and in a few minutes the game was going to start. Even though the team had just spent a half hour warming up, Polly still had goose bumps thinking about the game ahead.

"Okay, guys, it's the first game of the season," the coach said when the team had gathered around. "Get out there and do your best. Just remember, it's great to win, but the most important thing is having fun."

"Yeah, right." Lukas snorted.

"What was that?" the coach asked, turning to him.

"I said, 'Right, Coach!'" Lukas replied brightly. But as soon as the coach looked away, he rolled his eyes.

Mike looked at Polly and shook his head. She knew he didn't like Lukas's attitude. Polly didn't like it much, either. *I might not be as good as Lukas, but at least I don't act like that,* she thought.

With a shout of "Go, team!" the huddle broke and the Devils headed for their positions. As Polly jogged onto the field, she looked over at the small crowd that had come to watch the game. She saw parents and grandparents, older kids and younger ones, but she didn't see anyone she knew.

At one end of the field, a little group of moms stood together, chatting. *They look like they know each other. I'll bet they come to all the games,* Polly thought with a pang. She wished that someone from her own family had come to see her play.

The ref blew his whistle, and the game kicked off. Polly was playing midfield, which meant she had to run a lot. For the first few minutes she forgot about everything as she chased after the ball.

The Devils had had plenty of scrimmages during practice. But that hadn't quite prepared Polly for a real game. Everything seemed to happen much faster. The ball switched sides so many times, Polly kept getting turned around.

"Let's go, defense! Hustle, Polly!" Coach Kleet called as the other team — the Wolverines — gained control of the ball again.

Polly turned and saw the Wolverines' striker coming right toward her. *This is my chance,* she thought.

As the striker moved forward, Polly stepped up to block him. She expected him to dodge right or left. Instead, he plowed right into her. Both players tumbled to the ground.

Polly didn't take her eyes off the ball. She saw it pop up into the air. Before Polly had time to think about it, she found herself jumping back up to meet it.

Polly looked down at her feet. She had the ball! She'd stolen it right out from under the Wolverines' striker!

"Go, Polly! Go! Kick the ball!"

Polly heard her teammates screaming her name. She looked around for someone to pass to. That's when she saw the Wolverines' goal. It was wide open.

Quickly, before she missed her chance, Polly kicked the ball toward the goal with all her might.

It was a perfect kick, even better than the one she'd sent over Mike's fence. Polly heard the other players gasp in admiration. *I've got it!* she thought. *I'm going to score!*

She saw a blur of red and white as the goalie leaped up to try to block the shot.

Wait . . . red and white? Polly thought. *That's not the Wolverines' goalie. That's . . .*

OUR goalie!

The next few seconds seemed to happen in slow motion. Polly saw the ball brush against the goalie's fingertips. She saw the goalie grimace. She saw her teammates clutch their heads. Their lips moved, but she couldn't hear any sounds come out.

Then the ball flew into the net.

For a moment there was a stunned silence. Without waiting for the referee's whistle, Polly turned and walked off the field.

A second later the whistle came. The ref called halftime.

The Devils gathered around the water cooler. Polly could feel her teammates staring at her, but she couldn't meet their eyes.

Finally, Coach Kleet cleared her throat. "What happened out there, Polly?"

Polly just shrugged. She was afraid if she opened her mouth to speak, she might start to cry.

"Do you realize you scored against *your own team*?" Lukas snapped. "That's the dumbest thing you can do!"

"That's enough, Lukas. Let's leave Polly alone for a little bit." The coach steered him and the rest of the team away.

"Are you okay?" Mike asked Polly when the other kids were gone.

Polly shook her head. On the other side of the field, she could see some Wolverines pointing at her and laughing. The players' parents were all staring at her, too. She could see them putting their heads together and whispering. *I can just imagine what they're saying about me,* Polly thought.

But . . . wait. Polly looked closer. They weren't looking at her, after all. They were staring at something *behind* her.

Just then, Polly heard a familiar voice call, "Yoo-hoo!"

Polly whirled around. There stood Veronica. She wore an old-fashioned high-necked dress and elbow-length gloves, and her long black hair was piled high on her head. She carried a black umbrella as if it was a cane. On the soccer field, Veronica was a strange sight indeed. Polly had never been so happy to see her.

"What are you doing here?" she asked, hurrying over. "I thought you had the blood drive."

Veronica waved a hand. "Oh, blood. Who really needs it? I couldn't miss my step-daughter's first soccer game, could I?"

"Is Dad here, too?" Polly asked, looking around.

"No, he couldn't make it. You know he would have, if he could," Veronica said.

"I'm glad he's not here," Polly said, her eyes suddenly filling with tears. "I never should have started soccer. I'm the worst player ever."

"That's not true! I arrived just in time to see you kick the ball into that . . . er, web thingy." With the tip of her umbrella, Veronica pointed to the Devils' goal.

"It's called a net," Polly told her. "*Our* net. I scored a goal . . . against my own team!" She began to sob.

"Oh, dearest. Come here." Veronica held open her arms, and Polly stepped into them. Veronica might have been the oddest mother in the world, but her hugs were as good as any.

"I really thought I could be good at soccer," Polly said sadly, when she'd at last caught her breath. "But the truth is, I stink." She wiped her eyes. "Anyway, at least you're here. So now we can go home."

"Home?" Veronica looked at the other players. Halftime was over and they'd started returning to the field. "But the game isn't over yet, is it?"

"It doesn't matter," Polly said. "I'm quitting soccer."

"Quitting?" Veronica's brow furrowed.

Then she shook her head. "I'm afraid that won't do."

"What do you mean?" Polly asked in alarm.

"Please go tell your coach that you'd like her to put you back in," Veronica said, in a voice that left no room for argument. Then, more gently, she added, "You don't know what might happen if you give it another chance."

Polly thought she saw a strange glimmer in Veronica's green eyes. But a second later it was gone.

Feeling a pit in her stomach, Polly trudged over to Coach Kleet and told her she wanted to go back in.

The coach studied her. "Are you sure?"

Polly glanced over her shoulder at Veronica, who gave her a brisk nod. Polly sighed and turned back to the coach. "I'm sure."

"No way!" cried Lukas, overhearing them. "You can't put Polly back in. She's death on the field."

"Zip it, Lukas. I make the decisions around here," the coach said. "Polly, I want you at left-wing defense. And I expect you to look sharp, you hear?"

Polly nodded.

Back on the field, Polly watched the kick-off anxiously. "Just stay away from the ball," she told herself. "If you don't touch the ball, nothing bad can happen."

No sooner had the words left her lips than she saw the ball rolling straight toward her.

Polly panicked. She lashed out with her foot, kicking the ball away without even thinking where it would go. To her surprise, it sailed straight up into the air.

Up, up, up the ball went, until it became just a dot against the sky.

A second later, it came hurtling back down. It landed right in front of the Wolverines' goal. The surprised goalie didn't have time to react. The ball slipped past him and rolled into the net.

For a second, there was a stunned silence. Then the crowd exploded in cheers.

"Go, Polly!" the Devils screamed. Coach Kleet whooped and waved her visor in the air.

As Polly passed Mike, they high-fived. "What'd I tell you?" he said. "You're a natural!"

Polly grinned, suddenly feeling a surge of confidence.

The rest of the game went much better. Polly didn't trip once, and she even gave a few good assists. By the end, the Devils had won, 4–3.

"Way to turn things around, Polly," Coach Kleet said as the Devils celebrated their victory with soda and energy bars. "I knew you could do it! You just had to get your head in the game."

Veronica seemed just as proud as if she'd scored the goal herself. "That was exhilarating," she told Polly as they headed home together. "I never knew soccer could be so much fun."

Polly beamed. "Thanks, Veronica. I'm really glad I stuck it out after all. When I scored that goal, it felt so good."

"I know just what you mean, dear," Veronica said, and her strange green eyes twinkled.

❖ Chapter 5 ❖

I'm so excited. I've been looking forward to this game all week!" Veronica said as she piloted the car down the street.

It had been a week since the Devils' victory over the Wolverines. Today they were up against a new team, the Tigers. Veronica was driving Polly to her game, and this time Polly's dad was coming, too. He was riding up in the front seat, next to Veronica.

"I've been doing a bit of reading about soccer," Veronica continued. "It's a very sophisticated sport. Did you know that one national soccer team hired a witch doctor to cure a losing streak?"

"I guess they were hoping to get ahead . . . a *shrunken* head, that is!" Dr. Winkler joked.

Polly sat in the backseat, barely listening to the conversation. Her mind was on the game. After their victory the week before, Polly had been certain that her soccer skills were getting better. But all week at practice, she'd played badly. Polly was starting to wonder if her incredible kick had just been an accident.

Her dad twisted around in the seat to look at her. "Almost there. How ya doing, champ?"

"Great, Dad," Polly said, trying to ignore the butterflies in her stomach. She wanted to play well that day, so her dad would be proud of her.

"I was sorry I missed your big goal last week," Dr. Winkler said. "That's why I brought the video camera. This time, I won't miss a thing!"

Polly smiled weakly. She hoped she didn't score against her own team again. She certainly didn't need a video of *that*.

As they pulled into the parking lot, Polly could see her team warming up on the field. "I'd better get going," Polly said, climbing out of the car. "I'm already late."

She turned to say good-bye to her parents, then stopped. "Veronica? What are you wearing?"

"Do you like it?" Veronica asked. Over the top of her dress, she had on a T-shirt that read GO DEVILS! It had a picture of a soccer ball with little red horns and a tail of fire. "I made it myself," she told Polly.

"Wow," Polly said. "That's cool!"

"You look like a real soccer fan!" Dr. Winkler agreed.

"Go, Devils!" Veronica shouted so loudly that Polly jumped. "Let's get out there and score some goals!"

Polly's dad laughed. "You even *sound* like a fan. Come on," he said, taking her hand, "let's get some good seats. See you after the game, Polly."

Polly waved and headed off to join her team.

"Well, look who it is," Lukas sneered as she ran up. "Polly Blooper, the biggest loser in soccer history."

"Lay off, Lukas," Mike said angrily. "In case you forgot, she scored an awesome goal in our last game."

"Correction," said Lukas. "She scored *two* goals. And one was for the other team."

Polly scowled. "You think you're so smart, Lukas."

"Smart enough to know which goal is mine," Lukas replied, and sauntered away.

"Forget it, Polly," Mike said, putting a hand on her shoulder. "He's the kind of player that gives soccer a bad name."

But Polly was still steaming. *Just you wait, Lukas,* she thought. *I'll show you how I can really play.*

I just hope I play okay, she added nervously.

But Polly needn't have worried. From the moment after the kickoff, she could tell that she was on top of her game. Right away, she stole the ball from a Tiger midfielder and took it up the field. Dribbling had never seemed so easy!

"Polly!"

Hearing her name, Polly looked up. She saw Lukas signaling for her to pass the ball. But Polly didn't want to pass to Lukas. She looked around for someone else.

Far up the field, Mike was open. But there were several players between them. Still, if Polly could boot the ball all the way upfield, she just might make it.

Should I risk it? she wondered. She decided to try. Rearing back her foot, Polly drove her toe into the ball as hard as she could.

But she didn't quite land the kick. Instead of flying into the air, the ball went zipping away across the ground. "Uh-oh," Polly groaned. It was headed right for the Tigers' defense!

A Tiger fullback pounced. But at the last second, the ball swerved out of the way. It zigzagged between the surprised players like a skier on a slalom course.

"He's got it!" Polly said as Mike stepped up to receive the pass.

But the ball didn't stop at Mike. It

bounced right over the top of Mike's foot and rolled into the Tigers' goal.

For a second, Polly wasn't sure what had happened. "Did I score a goal?"

The sound of cheering answered her question. "Yeah, Polly!" her teammates shouted.

Polly looked into the crowd and saw her dad and Veronica waving. Veronica punched the air with her fist. "Devils are number one!" she screeched.

As the Devils ran back up the field, Polly passed Mike. She slapped him a high five. "I meant to pass it to you," she said.

"You didn't need me. That shot was unbelievable!" Mike shook his head in amazement. "You never did anything like that in practice."

"I guess it's like you said. Everything's different in a real game." Polly laughed when she saw Lukas's stunned expression. "I guess he doesn't seem so smart now."

That first play seemed to give Polly the confidence she needed. The rest of the game, she was unstoppable. She scored three more goals, and even landed a bicycle kick — kicking the ball backward over her head, something Polly didn't even know she could do.

By the end of the game, the Devils had won 5–0. The team was so excited, they lifted Polly onto their shoulders. She'd never been so proud of herself.

After the game, her dad swept her up in a big bear hug. "You were amazing, kiddo!" he exclaimed.

"We really showed those Tigers!" Veronica chimed in.

"Thanks, Veroni —" Polly broke off. Her stepmother looked very strange. Veronica's usually smooth black hair was a wild cloud around her face. Her cheeks were flushed, and her eyes glittered oddly.

"Doesn't it feel great to score a goal? It really gets the heart racing," Veronica said. She sounded out of breath, as if she'd been running.

"Er —" Polly frowned. Something was weird. . . .

"I caught every single play on video!" her dad exclaimed before Polly could finish her thought.

"Excuse me." A man standing nearby tapped Dr. Winkler on the shoulder. "Did you say you got the game on film?"

"Right here!" Dr. Winkler held up his video camera.

"I'm a sportscaster on Channel Thirteen," the man said, handing Polly's dad his card. "I'd love to show some of that footage on the evening news. I've never seen anything like it. Your daughter has an incredible talent." He smiled down at Polly.

"You hear that, Polly?" her dad said. "You're going to be on the news!"

Polly grinned, her worries fading away. She couldn't believe it. This was turning out to be the best day of her life!

✤ Chapter 6 ✤

That evening, Polly's entire family gathered in the living room to watch the news.

"Hurry, Dad! We're going to miss it!" Polly cried as she took a seat on the bearskin rug.

"We're not going to miss it." Dr. Winkler looked around, scratching his head. "Now, where could that channel changer be?"

"You mean the one with the big red button?" asked Damon, who was sitting on the claw-foot sofa between Vincent and Esme. "I may have rewired it to be a short-range missile launcher."

"Damon, please stop joking around," Dr. Winkler said as Esme pulled the remote out from between the sofa cushions. Dr. Winkler took it and pushed a button. They heard a whistling sound, followed by a distant boom.

"Yep," said Damon. "That's the one."

"Oh, for goodness' sake. We don't have time for this," said Joy, hopping up from a bat-shaped chair. "Polly's going to be on TV!"

Joy flipped through the channels on the television until she found the right one. Polly recognized the man who had been at her soccer game. He was wearing a suit and tie and sitting at a news desk. "Now for today's sports news," he said. "A local girl turns out to be a soccer phenomenon."

"Phenomenon," said Petey. "P-h-e —"

"Shhhh!" everyone said.

"Today in a community league game,

ten-year-old Polly Winkler made a shot never before seen in soccer history," the sportscaster announced. "Let's take a look."

They cut to a clip of Polly's soccer game. Polly watched herself kick the ball, then followed its path as it zigzagged up the field and landed in the Tigers' goal.

"That's my video!" Dr. Winkler said proudly.

"Incredible, isn't it?" said the sportscaster. "Let's slow it down."

They watched the play again in slow motion. "She doesn't even put a spin on the ball," the sportscaster commented. "How does she do it?"

They cut to a shot of Polly being interviewed. "I don't know," Polly said into the microphone. "I just kick the ball and it goes in."

The sportscaster chuckled. "What a modest young lady," he said, smiling at the camera. "This girl has an almost supernatural talent."

"Supernatural?" murmured Vincent, frowning. "Mother —"

"Shhh!" Veronica cut him off. "I want to hear this!"

"One thing's for sure," the sportscaster was saying as they played Polly's kick again. "This young soccer star has a very bright future ahead."

"Yaaay!" Joy cheered, flipping the TV off. "Polly, you're a star!"

"What? No sacrifice?" Esme asked, scowling at the blank TV.

But the rest of the family was cheering and patting Polly on the back. For the second time that day, she felt like she might burst with pride.

"I'd say this calls for a celebration!" Veronica said. "Who wants a slice of mud pie? Fresh from the garden!"

"I do!" everyone cried. And with that they all piled into the kitchen to celebrate Polly's victory.

⟨✦✦✦⟩

Late that night, Polly's eyes snapped open. Her room was dark, except for a faint glow coming from her alarm clock. Something had awakened her.

The Kreeps' old mansion was full of odd noises — bats, mice, creaky floorboards, the sinister ticking of old clocks. But this noise was different. It sounded like the roar of a faraway river. It was coming from somewhere downstairs.

Polly climbed out of bed and crept down the stairs. The kitchen was quiet, and so was the dining room. As Polly passed the living room, she noticed a bluish, flickering light.

Polly tiptoed into the room. Someone had left the TV on. On the screen was a soccer game. The noise Polly had heard was the sound of the crowd cheering.

Polly was about to turn the TV off when a dark shape rose up from the couch. Polly screamed and flicked on a light.

"Veronica!" she cried.

"Hello, dear," Veronica said. "What are you doing up?"

"I heard a noise," Polly explained. "What are *you* doing? I thought you didn't like TV." Veronica usually avoided the television. She said it bothered her third eye.

"I didn't want to miss this game," Veronica told her. "The Super Eagles are playing the Indomitable Lions."

"But it's three in the morning!"

"It's noon in Cameroon," Veronica pointed out.

Wow, Polly thought. *Veronica is really*

59

getting into soccer. But Polly didn't mind. Being a super soccer mom was probably the most normal thing her stepmother had ever done!

She sat down on the couch next to her stepmother. "Who's winning?" she asked.

"The Lions," Veronica said. "Watch this one." She pointed to a player in a green jersey. He was running circles around the other team's defense. He moved so gracefully, he looked like he was dancing.

"Wow!" said Polly. "He's like a ball magnet!"

"Ball magnet?" Veronica arched a thin eyebrow. "What does that mean?"

"You know, the ball sticks to him wherever he goes. Wow." She sighed. "It would be great to be able to play like that."

"Ball magnet," Veronica said thoughtfully. "Hmmm."

"What's going on in here?" asked a sleepy voice.

Polly and Veronica turned. Polly's dad was standing in the doorway. He was wearing rumpled pajamas, and his hair was sticking up all over his head. "Soccer?" he asked, looking at the TV in surprise. "At three in the morning?"

"It's noon in Cameroon," Polly pointed out.

"It's an important game!" Veronica added.

Dr. Winkler looked back and forth between them. "Well, then I guess I'd better not miss it," he said. He sat down on the couch next to Polly. "Who's winning?"

"The Lions," Polly told him.

As she snuggled happily between her dad and Veronica, Polly decided that taking up soccer was the best thing she'd ever done.

❊ Chapter 7 ❊

O kay, guys. I want everyone's attention," said Coach Kleet.

Hands on her hips, she looked over the team. It was Saturday morning, and the Devils were gathered for their pre-game pep talk. "Today I need you to be on your best defense," the coach told them. "We're up against some tough competition."

Lukas nodded. "The Parkside Puffins."

"The *Puffins*?" Polly giggled. "They don't sound very tough to me."

"Yeah? Well, I guess the great Polly Winkler doesn't know everything," Lukas snapped.

Polly sighed. Ever since her incredible play the week before, Lukas had been nastier than ever. *He's just jealous of my amazing natural talent,* Polly thought. *But can I help it if I'm awesome?*

She turned to Mike and asked, "What's Lukas talking about?"

"Them." Mike pointed across the field. A team in yellow shirts had just arrived. The players were the biggest kids Polly had ever seen!

"*Those* are the Puffins?" asked a boy next to Polly. He pointed to a tall girl with bright orange braids. "She looks like she should be in high school!"

"We're going to get creamed," Mike murmured.

But Polly was hardly paying attention. She had just noticed a large crowd of people gathered by the soccer field. "Why are all those people here?" she wondered aloud.

Mike gave her a funny look. "Don't you know? They're here to see you, Polly."

"Me?" Polly looked at the crowd again. Most were people she didn't recognize. A lot of them had video cameras. Polly wasn't sure whether to feel proud or scared. She'd never expected to get *this* much attention!

"I want you to be on extra-good defense," Coach Kleet was telling the team. "But most important, *keep passing*!"

Then, with a rallying cry of "Break!" she sent the team onto the field.

"Go, Polly!" she heard her dad and Veronica yelling. They had both come to the game. "Let's make pie out of those Puffins!" Veronica added.

As Polly lined up for the kickoff, she noticed that the giant orange-haired girl was right across from her. The girl narrowed her eyes and mouthed, "You're dead meat."

Polly gulped.

At the kickoff, the Puffins took control of the ball. Polly did her best to guard the orange-haired giant. But the girl was so much bigger, Polly felt like a kitten trying to guard a moose. Within moments, the Puffins had scored.

"Let's go, defense!" Coach Kleet shouted to the Devils.

"Get that ball," Polly told herself as the teams lined up again.

In the next play, Polly got her chance. The Puffins' fullback sent a long pass up the field. But halfway there, the ball suddenly curved. It landed right at Polly's feet!

Polly looked toward the Puffins' goal. It was totally walled in, except for a small gap to the left.

But the goalie is favoring the right side, Polly thought. *Maybe I still have a chance. . . .*

"Polly!" Mike yelled.

Polly saw that he was wide open. She looked back toward the goal. All she could see was a cluster of yellow shirts. The gap in the Puffins' defense had started to close.

Polly desperately wanted to score the first goal of the game. But she knew she didn't have a clear shot. What's more, the Puffins' orange-haired midfielder had turned and was charging toward Polly like an angry buffalo.

"Polly! I'm open!" Mike flailed his arms.

With a flash of regret, Polly sent the ball skidding across the grass to Mike.

The ball had only gone a few feet, though, when it gave a little jerk, as if it had come to the end of an invisible leash. It reversed direction and rolled back to Polly.

"Huh?" Polly blinked in surprise. But she didn't have time to wonder what happened. The orange-haired girl was almost

up to her. Polly could see bits of grass flying from the girl's churning cleats.

Polly closed her eyes and booted the ball as hard as she could.

"Oof!" she grunted as the girl barreled into her. They both hit the ground, hard.

When Polly opened her eyes, she saw the ball sailing through the air. With a groan, she realized her shot had gone wide. She'd missed the goal by a mile.

Then, to her amazement, the ball began to turn.

It drew a graceful half circle in the air and came down right in front of the Puffins' goal. The right-wing fullback ran up to stop it, but it bounced between his legs and rolled on toward the goal.

As the goalie knelt to scoop it up, the ball seemed to change course yet again. With a tiny swerve, it dodged the goalie's fingertips and rolled into the net.

The crowd exploded with cheers. Polly picked herself up off the ground. *I did it!* she thought. She wasn't quite sure *how* she'd done it, but at the moment it didn't matter.

The orange-haired girl stood up, too. She gave Polly a fierce look. "Impossible!"

"Says you!" replied Polly with a toss of her ponytail. Then she turned and ran back to her teammates.

The Devils were beside themselves. They whooped and shouted and slapped high fives.

"Awesome, Polly!"

"Too cool!"

"Way to go!"

"Bravo, darling! Absolutely devastating!"

Polly turned and saw her stepmother standing just beyond the end line. Today she looked like a gypsy fortune-teller, with a bloodred scarf tied over her hair and big, dangly hoop earrings. Beneath a fringed black shawl, she was wearing her GO DEVILS! T-shirt. When she caught Polly's eye, she winked.

Suddenly, Polly felt uneasy.

She looked back at the Puffins' goal, where the players were still shaking their heads in disbelief. A phrase from the sportscaster's news report popped into her mind: *an almost supernatural talent.*

That shot was impossible, Polly thought. *So how did I make it?*

Could it have been more than just good luck and mad soccer skills?

Could it have been — magic?

"Polly!" Coach Kleet's voice jolted her out of her thoughts. "You put quite a spin on that ball!"

Polly grinned. The coach was right! What did she have to worry about? She'd just pulled off an awesome maneuver. "No sweat, Coach," she said. "It was easy!"

But the coach didn't look happy. "This isn't the game for fancy shots," she told Polly. "We're here to play soccer, not show off."

"But the ball went in!" Polly protested.

"I told you to keep passing, and I meant it," the coach said, and walked away.

"Jeez." Polly turned to Mike. "What's up with her?"

"I was open," Mike replied with a scowl.

"Huh?"

"I was open," Mike repeated. "You should have passed to me."

"I did! I mean . . . I *tried*," Polly stammered, "but the ball sort of rolled back and . . . Anyway, who cares? We scored!"

Mike folded his arms. He still looked angry. "You're supposed to pass. It's called *teamwork*."

Polly laughed. "You're starting to sound like Coach Kleet."

"Well *you're* starting to sound like Lukas," Mike snapped. He turned and walked away.

Polly felt stung. *What's bugging him?* she wondered. Was it possible that Mike was jealous of her, too?

One thing's for sure, she thought as she headed back out to the field. *There's a lot more to soccer than just kicking.*

For the next quarter of the game, Polly made an extra effort to pass to her teammates. But no matter how hard she tried, she just couldn't do it. The ball would only go a few feet before it rolled back to her.

Mike wasn't the only one who was getting annoyed. Before long, all her teammates were calling Polly a "ball hog."

71

"Pass the ball!" they screamed again and again.

Polly tried. She really did. But the ball always came back to her, as if drawn by a magnet.

Passing wasn't Polly's only problem. The Puffins' orange-haired midfielder was also sticking to Polly like glue. Wherever Polly went, the girl went, too. And she played rough! She used elbows and knees, and more than once Polly got her foot crushed beneath the girl's big cleats.

"Is that ref *blind*?" Polly complained to Mike when it happened again. "Why doesn't he call a foul?"

"Maybe he would if you weren't such a *ball hog*," Mike snapped.

Polly sighed. She was starting to feel like no one was on her side. Except for her family, of course — especially Veronica.

"Marvelous, darling!" Veronica exclaimed

at halftime. "We're going to win this game single-handedly!"

"If I even make it through the game," Polly grumbled, rubbing a bruise on her arm. "That midfielder thinks I'm her personal punching bag."

"Is that so?" Veronica narrowed her eyes at the orange-haired girl. "It sounds like she needs to learn some manners."

In the second half of the game, the Puffins seemed more determined than ever. Even Polly could hardly get near the ball. Within a few moments, they'd already made an attempt on the Devils' goal. Luckily, the goalie blocked the shot.

The goalie dropkicked the ball and sent it sailing back to the field.

"Got it!" Polly yelled as it came toward her.

Just then, the orange-haired girl stepped in front of her. The girl was so tall she blocked out the sky. Polly knew she planned to head the ball, and there was nothing Polly could do. She couldn't get around her. And she sure as heck couldn't out-jump her.

But just as the ball reached them, the girl let out a bloodcurdling scream. She ducked, and the ball hit Polly squarely in the chest. It bounced off and rolled to a stop.

Wheeeeeet! The ref's whistle split the air.

The Puffins' coach rushed onto the field. He hurried over to the orange-haired girl. She was on the ground with her face in her hands.

"What happened?" the coach asked. He cast an accusing glance at Polly.

"I didn't do anything!" Polly told him. As the ref walked up, Polly added, "I didn't touch her."

The coach and the ref ignored her. They

hovered over the orange-haired girl, asking, "Are you okay? Are you hurt?"

"It was horrible!" the girl wailed.

"Can you stand?" the coach asked.

The girl looked up at them. "Horrible," she repeated. "That ball . . . it was a *skull!*"

❄ **Chapter 8** ❄

Just calm down, Heather," the Puffins' coach said. He helped the orange-haired girl to her feet. "Now, tell us what happened."

Heather sniffled and wiped her nose on the back of her hand. "I was going to block the shot," she said in a wobbly voice. "But when I jumped up to head the ball, it wasn't a ball anymore. It was a skull! It was grinning at me in this evil way."

The coach and the ref exchanged a look. The ref walked over to the ball and picked it up. He turned it over in his hands, inspecting every side. Then he looked at the coach and shook his head.

The Puffins' coach sighed. "Why don't you take a rest, Heather? You can sit this one out," he said. He put an arm around her shoulders and started to steer her toward the sidelines.

"But I did see a skull. I know I did," Polly heard Heather whine as they walked away.

"Did you foul her?" Lukas asked, coming up next to Polly.

"No." Polly frowned. "She thought the ball turned into a skull."

"Seriously?" Lukas laughed. "What a nutcase!"

"I guess," Polly said. But she didn't feel like laughing. Her confidence had been replaced by a creeping feeling of doubt.

Polly looked over at her stepmother. Was it her imagination or was there a sly smile tugging at the corners of Veronica's mouth?

At that moment, Coach Kleet called Polly off the field. "What is it, Coach?" asked Polly, jogging over to her.

"You'll sit this one out. I'm putting Jesika in," the coach told her.

"What?" Polly exclaimed. "You can't take me out. I didn't do anything!"

"You haven't been playing like a team player," the coach said.

"But we're winning!" Polly argued.

"You can't take her out. We're winning!" echoed a voice behind them.

Polly and the coach turned. Veronica was standing there with her arms folded and a scowl on her face.

"Who are you?" Coach Kleet asked.

Veronica lifted her chin proudly. "I'm her stepmother."

"Well, *I'm* the coach," said Coach Kleet. "And I don't like your daughter's attitude."

"Attitude?" Veronica huffed. Her green eyes glittered dangerously. "I'll tell you something about attitude!"

Suddenly, a soccer ball, which had been lying near Polly's feet, popped up in the air . . . and smacked the coach in the nose!

A gasp arose from the crowd. Polly gasped, too. "That wasn't me!" she tried to say. "I didn't —"

"Pipe down!" roared the coach. Her face was red with anger. "You are out for the rest of this game!"

As the coach stormed away, Polly plopped down miserably on the bench. She hadn't kicked that ball into the coach's nose. But she had a feeling she knew who had.

"Benched!" Veronica huffed, coming to stand next to Polly. "That coach will be sorry. The Devils don't stand a chance of winning now!"

Polly sighed and put her head in her hands. Somehow this soccer thing had gotten completely out of control!

✷ Chapter 9 ✷

The ride home from the game that day was a quiet one. After a few blocks, Dr. Winkler gently ventured, "Well, that was quite a game. But Polly, sweetie, maybe you shouldn't have kicked that ball at the coach —"

"She deserved it!" Veronica snapped. "A one-eyed toad could coach better than her."

After that, no one said anything.

As soon as she got home, Polly locked herself in her room. She paced back and forth, going over the strange events of the day.

First, there had been her amazing kick. ("Not just amazing," Polly reminded herself. *"Impossible."*) Then there had been the magnetic ball and the mysterious skull, not to mention the ball that had jumped up and bopped Coach Kleet in the nose.

Polly could only think of one explanation for all those things: magic. And she only knew one person who could do that kind of magic: Veronica. Polly had always suspected that her stepmother was a witch, even though she'd never been able to prove it.

Polly flopped down on her bed. She wondered if she could just be imagining things. She'd always been told she had a big imagination.

But the more she thought about it, the more Polly was sure she was right. Hadn't she been a crummy soccer player — until Veronica showed up at her game? And wasn't it strange that Veronica had suddenly become such a big soccer fan?

But not just a regular fan, Polly thought. Veronica was actually *playing* the game — and pretending the moves were Polly's!

"That does it!" Polly hopped up from her bed and marched across the room. "I'm going to tell Veronica to cut it out. Soccer is *my* game!"

But at the door, she slowed. If Veronica stopped helping her, then Polly wouldn't be a soccer star anymore. No one would think she was amazing. No one would come to her games. No one would hug her and tell her they were proud.

She would go back to being plain old Polly.

Polly sighed and sat back down. Maybe she shouldn't say anything yet.

I have to think about the Devils, too, Polly reasoned. That day, the final score had been

7–2. Without Polly in the game, the Devils hadn't made a single goal. The Puffins had pulverized them.

"I'll stick it out until the end of the season," Polly decided. After the Devils had won the championship, she could quit.

It seemed like a pretty good plan. *I just hope I can wait that long,* Polly thought.

❖ Chapter 10 ❖

The next Saturday morning, Polly sat at the kitchen table, dawdling over breakfast.

"Eat up, kiddo!" her dad said. "You'll need energy for your big game today."

Polly prodded her cold eggs with a fork. She wasn't hungry. The thought of the soccer game made her stomach churn.

All week, Polly had been dreading the game. Who knew what kind of weird things would happen? She wasn't even excited about scoring a goal, now that she knew it wasn't her own doing.

Finally, Polly put her fork down. "I guess we'd better go," she said with a sigh. "Where's Veronica?"

"Didn't she tell you?" asked her dad, who was loading the dishwasher. "Joy is cheering at a big game this morning. Veronica and Esme went to watch."

"WHAT?" Polly leaped up, knocking over her chair. "You mean, she's not taking me to my game?"

"Don't worry. I'll drive you in the station wagon," her dad said.

"No, Dad — I need Veronica!" Polly cried. "She *has* to come to my game!"

Her dad shut the dishwasher and turned to her with a frown. "Polly, don't be selfish. Veronica has come to all your games. Now it's Joy's turn. Don't you think your sisters deserve some attention, too?"

Polly's head was spinning. If Veronica

wasn't there to do her magic, then Polly would go back to being normal.

No, Polly thought. *Not just normal. The WORST player on the soccer team!*

"Dad, suddenly I don't feel so good," she said, sitting back down.

"Don't be silly. You were fine just a second ago," said her dad. "Now go get your jacket. We're going to be late."

Polly got up from the chair feeling numb. There was no way around it. She was going to have to play.

And it was going to be a disaster.

"Golly, look at that crowd!" said her dad as they arrived at the soccer field. "It's even bigger than last week!"

Polly groaned inwardly. She'd hoped that after last week's trouble not many people would show up to this game. But they had come out in droves. It seemed the only thing more interesting than a soccer phenomenon was a soccer phenomenon with a bad attitude.

"Good luck, champ," Dr. Winkler said as they got out of the car. "Make your dad proud."

Polly swallowed hard. "Sure thing." Shoulders slumped, she turned and slowly headed toward the field.

"You're late," Coach Kleet said. She eyed Polly over her clipboard. "I don't want any hotshot moves today. You think you can manage that?"

"I don't think that's going to be a problem," Polly said miserably.

The coach nodded. "Good. Then I'm putting you in at right forward."

Ugh, thought Polly. Her last hope — that

she might be benched through the game — had just been dashed.

As she walked onto the field, Polly scanned the crowd. She hoped that Veronica had decided to turn up after all. But all she saw were strangers who had come to see her play.

At the kickoff, Mike stole the ball. He and Lukas passed it back and forth, taking it upfield, then passed it to Polly to score. Polly sent the ball flying . . . right out of bounds.

"What did you do that for?" Mike asked, bewildered.

"I didn't mean to!" Polly said honestly.

The game started again. The next time Polly got the ball, she tripped over it and sprawled on the ground.

"Polly, quit messing around and play!" Lukas snapped.

"I'm trying," Polly said. As she stood up, she could feel everyone watching her. She knew what they were saying: Polly Winkler, the soccer star, was a great big flop.

The rest of the game was just as bad. Her teammates kept passing her the ball, hoping that she would score. But Polly's shots seemed to go everywhere *but* the goal. Finally, the Devils changed their strategy. Instead of passing Polly the ball, they tried to keep it away from her.

Polly had to hand it to her teammates. Despite her mistakes, they were playing a good game. By the end of the fourth quarter, the score was tied 2–2.

The game went into overtime. But still neither team scored a goal. At last it was decided that the match would be settled with a penalty kick.

The other team went first. The kick sent the ball sailing through the air . . . to land in the arms of the Devils' goalie. The Devils all breathed a sigh of relief.

Just then, Polly heard a familiar voice screech, "Go, Devils!"

She spun around. There stood Veronica, wearing her Devils T-shirt and waving both hands in the air. The rest of Polly's family was there, too — Joy, Petey, Esme. Even Vincent and Damon. They had all come to see her.

Polly felt a flood of relief. With Veronica there, Polly knew she could save the game. She hurried over to Coach Kleet and tugged on her sleeve. "Coach, let me take the kick."

The coach frowned. "Polly, this is important. This shot is going to decide who wins."

Polly lifted her chin. "I know. I can do it."

To Polly's surprise, Mike stepped forward. "Let her do it," he told the coach.

"You can't be serious?" Lukas exclaimed. "Polly couldn't hit the side of a school bus!"

The coach ignored him. She looked back and forth between Mike and Polly. "Okay," she said finally. "Polly, you're in. But you'd better know what you're doing."

"Don't worry, Coach," Polly replied.

As she lined up for the penalty kick, she could feel the tension in the air. But Polly felt totally calm. She didn't doubt that the ball would go in. Polly glanced over at the crowd and sought out Veronica's eyes. Veronica gave her a small nod.

Polly nodded back. Then she took a deep breath and booted the ball.

The ball arced through the air. For a second, it looked like it might hit the goal-post. But it slipped past and dropped into the net. Just as Polly knew it would.

"We won! We won!" Polly's teammates jumped up and down. The crowd was cheering, too. On the sidelines, Polly could see Petey and Joy doing some cheer they'd made up.

Polly was glad that the Devils had won. But she didn't feel proud like she had when she'd scored the other goals. She knew she didn't really deserve the credit.

After the game, Veronica was the first one to hug her. "Congratulations, darling! You must be so happy."

Polly shrugged. "I guess."

"Hmm." Veronica studied her. "You don't look like someone who just won a game. What's wrong?"

Polly kicked at the grass. "I'm not the soccer star everyone thinks I am. I'm really no good at all."

"That's not true!" said Veronica.

"Yes, it is! And you know it," Polly said, suddenly angry. "I was a crummy soccer player, until *you* started coming to my games. But what I don't understand is why you care if I win."

"Oh, Polly." Veronica sighed. "That first day, you seemed so discouraged. I wanted to support you! And then it was so much fun to win. All the crowds and the cheering . . . I guess I got a little carried away. But you don't have to worry," she added quickly. "After last week I decided that I wouldn't get involved anymore."

"Except for today," Polly reminded her. "The last goal?"

Veronica looked surprised. "But that was all *you*, darling."

"Me?" Polly's eyes widened as it suddenly dawned on her. "You mean I scored that goal all on my own?"

Veronica nodded. "You did indeed. And I couldn't have done it better myself," she added with a wink.

Just then, the rest of the family came over. Polly's dad swept her up in a big bear hug. "I'm so proud of you."

"For winning?" Polly asked.

"For not giving up. That was a tough game, but you stuck it out. That's my Polly."

Polly hugged her dad tight.

"You seem taller," said her dad when he set her down. He stepped back and studied her. "Have you grown?"

Polly grinned. "Yep. An inch!"

"One whole inch?" Her dad whistled. "I'd say that calls for a celebration. Who wants ice cream?"

"I do!" cried Polly. "Can Mike come, too?" she added, remembering how her friend had stood up for her. She realized she hadn't been the best friend to Mike lately. She wanted to make it up to him.

"Of course," said Polly's dad. "Where is he?"

"I'll get him!" Polly said. She turned to leave, then stopped. "Hey, aren't those the two policemen from the graveyard?"

Two men in blue uniforms were making their way over to them.

"Hello, Officers," Polly's dad said cheerfully. "What's new? Did Vincent perform another heroic deed?"

"Actually, we're here about your other son, Damon," said one of the policemen.

"Damon's a hero?" Dr. Winkler asked, surprised.

"No, sir," the officer said grimly. "We believe your son Damon has been setting off dummy missiles all over the county. Apparently, he's been hacking into NASA's computer systems to get information."

Veronica beamed. "You see? I *knew* he was a genius!"

"I'm afraid we'll have to take him in for questioning," said the other policeman. "Do you know where he is?"

Polly looked around and caught a glimpse of Damon disappearing into the crowd. Normally she would have been glad that her troublemaking stepbrother was finally getting caught. But right now she was too happy.

"Nope," said Polly. "Haven't seen him."

"I'm sure he'll turn up eventually," Veronica added.

"Well, let us know when he does," the policeman said.

Polly quickly found Mike. As the family made their way to the car, Joy pulled Polly aside. "Polly," she whispered. "I have to talk to you."

"What is it?" Polly asked.

Joy licked her lips nervously. "You know how you're always talking about silly things, like magic and witchcraft? And I always said all that stuff is in your imagination?"

Polly nodded.

"Well, I know this sounds weird, but . . ." Joy lowered her voice. "Today at the football game, my pom-poms were doing some *very strange things*!"

Polly smiled and linked her arm through Joy's. "You don't say?"

❋ Epilogue ❋

Polly dribbled down the field, aiming for the middle of the goal. The goalie was standing tall in the center. But Polly thought she might be able to fake him out.

But the opposition's defender was breathing down her neck. So instead of shooting, Polly caught the ball with the inside of her foot and passed it to her team's center striker.

"Heads up, Veronica!" she cried.

Lifting the hem of her long skirt, Veronica fielded the pass. She dribbled toward the goal, which had been marked by two trash cans in the family's backyard. Veronica's long black hair streamed out behind her like a banner. Her mouth stretched wide in a grin.

"Honey, I'm open!" Polly's dad called to her from near the goal.

Veronica ignored him and charged on. She hadn't made it far, though, when a kamikaze yell split the air. A small shape appeared out of nowhere, hurtling toward Veronica.

A second later, Veronica and Esme were lying in a heap on the ground.

"Geez, Esme." Polly reached out a hand to help her up. "You're not supposed to *tackle* in soccer."

"Soccer?" Esme scowled. "I thought we were playing *pitz.*"

"Hey, what's going on down there?" Damon called from the far end of the lawn, where he was guarding the other goal. "I'm getting bored!"

"You're supposed to be *glad* that the ball is at the other end of the field," Polly hollered back to him.

"Well, something better happen soon or I'm going back to my laboratory," Damon threatened. "I have countries to dominate, you know."

Polly's dad was helping Veronica to her feet. "I believe that was a clear foul by Esme. I'd be happy to take the penalty kick for our team."

"Not on your life," Veronica told him. "*I'm* the one that got fouled. *I* get to take the penalty kick."

"You're turning into a real ball hog," Dr. Winkler said to his wife, giving her a kiss on the cheek.

"I know." Veronica beamed. "Isn't it wonderful?"

She went to the center of the lawn and set up for the penalty kick. In the goal box, Petey pushed up his glasses and bravely squared his shoulders.

Thwunk! Veronica gave the ball a good, hard boot. Petey squealed and covered his head with his hands. But he needn't have worried. The shot went wide.

"Awwww!" everyone groaned.

But then, just as the ball was about to skim past the goalpost, it stopped. Suddenly, it reversed direction and rolled into the goal.

Veronica pumped the air with her fist. "Yesss!"

"That was quite a shot, honey!" said Polly's dad.

"Yaaaaaay!" Joy cheered, kicking her leg in the air.

Vincent shook his head at Joy. "What are you cheering about? She's not even on your team."

"I know," Joy replied. "But I love to see people win!"

Polly's dad stared at the goal, scratching his head. "I'm still not sure how that shot went in," he said.

Looking at Veronica, Polly thought she saw a twinkle in those emerald green eyes. She was pretty sure she knew how Veronica had made the goal. But she wasn't going to tell.

After all, Polly thought, *I guess a little bit of magic never hurt.*

Meet the Kreeps

Check out the whole spooky series!

#1: There Goes the Neighborhood

#2: The New Step-Mummy

#3: The Nanny Nightmare

#4: The Mad Scientist

#5: Three's a Krowd

#6: Kicking and Screaming

For more magical fun, be sure to check out these tails of enchantment!